Intruder

The Intruder

R. C. LINDQUIST ● CHRIS JOHNSTON

FRANKLIN WATTS
NEW YORK ● LONDON ● SYDNEY

This edition published in 1999 by
Franklin Watts
96 Leonard Street
London EC2A 4XD

Published 1997 by
Thomas C. Lothian Pty Ltd, Australia

Series Editor: Gary Crew

A CIP catalogue record for this book
is available from the British Library.

ISBN 0 7496 3597 5

Printed in Guernsey

Contents

Chapter **One**

Taryn waved and her mother bipped the horn as she drove off. Mrs Hewitt was in a good mood because Taryn's sister had come home with the news that she'd found a holiday job. Taryn's mother ran her own business and didn't give pocket money. According to her, you had to learn the value of money by working for it.

That's why Taryn was here to babysit

Mrs Garrance's four year old.

Taryn looked up at the trendy townhouse and saw a pale little face watching from the second-storey window. She lifted her hand in a jaunty wave. The child gave a guilty jerk, as if caught out, and disappeared. Poor kid, Taryn thought. Scared of her own shadow.

She ran lightly up the steps to the front door and knocked. The first thing she noticed when the door swung open was the security camera which swivelled toward her.

Mrs Garrance was the Assistant Director of P.R.D. – whatever *that* meant. She wore a smart business suit and a worried expression.

'You must be Taryn Hewitt. Come in.' Mrs Garrance glanced up the stairwell and lowered her voice. 'This is the first time I've left my daughter alone at night and she's playing up. Serendipity has had her bath and her dinner and she's promised to be on her best behaviour. Everything *should* be all right. But ...'

Taryn smiled – how much trouble could one four year old be? As a seasoned babysitter she'd

learnt to deal with Anxious Mothers and Four-Year-Old Tantrums. 'Not a problem, Mrs Garrance. I'm used to little kids. My brother has just turned five. If I can look after him, I can look after anyone!'

Taryn was used to people smiling when she said this, but Mrs Garrance just pursed her lips and looked grim. 'Serendipity is very advanced for her age. Come up and I'll introduce you.'

Taryn grinned. 'Is she Serena for short, or just Dipity?'

Mrs Garrance stopped midway on the stairs, her face perfectly straight. 'I always call her Serendipity.'

'Oh.'

No sense of humour, Taryn decided, and nervous too. As if to confirm this she noticed another security camera over the stairwell.

Serendipity's mother led Taryn down the short hall to the back bedroom. When the door opened, a little girl with pale blond hair looked up from the bed where she'd been playing with her stuffed toys.

Taryn noticed that Mrs Garrance walked over but didn't sit on the bed or hug her daughter.

'I have to go out to the department meeting now, Serendipity. This is Taryn, who's come to look after you. I don't want any nonsense.' Mrs Garrance's voice was very firm. 'You know what I mean?'

The little girl glanced resentfully at Taryn.

'Serendipity?' her mother insisted. 'You understand?'

The blond head nodded.

Taryn dropped to her heels, determined to win the child over. She glanced at the toys on the bed,

'Hi there, Serendipity. I have a little brother the same age as you and he has a bear just like that. Do you take him to bed with you?'

The little girl gave her a superior look. 'It is a stuffed toy. It doesn't need to sleep!'

Taryn's mouth dropped open.

Mrs Garrance smiled. 'My daughter has a Mensa level IQ, Taryn, fifty points above average. I don't indulge in any babyish nonsense with her. Now, let's go downstairs and I'll leave you my mobile phone number.' She gave the child a peck on the cheek. 'Good night, Miss, and no nonsense!'

Not a lot of affection there, Taryn thought, or maybe they weren't a demonstrative family. There was no mention of a Mr Garrance.

In the neat little blue and white kitchen Taryn listened to all the mother's instructions and nodded at the appropriate moments, though privately she thought it a bit severe.

No food once in bed, no night-light, no nonsense.

'If Serendipity has a bad dream, tell her it's all in her mind, tell her to exercise a little self-discipline. Whatever you do, don't *indulge* her.'

'Yes, Mrs G. – '

'It's Mrs Garrance, Taryn. I'm not a character from an American Sitcom.'

Taryn felt a resentful flush creep up her cheeks. She was glad the woman wasn't *her* mother!

'Now, the number of my mobile is next to the phone. You won't have any trouble if you follow my instructions. I'll be back around ten, as I told your mother.'

Chapter **Two**

With Mrs Garrance gone, Taryn made sure all the windows and doors were locked – she'd seen enough teen horror movies about babysitters to avoid the obvious mistakes – and went up to check on Serendipity.

The little girl was sitting on her bed playing intently with all the toys, which were spread out in rows.

At least Mrs Garrance allowed her to have toys, Taryn thought as she glanced around the room. She wrinkled her nose. What did a four-year-old want with her own computer?

Taryn sat on the end of the bed. 'Hi, Serena. What are you doing?'

'My name is Serendipity and I'm teaching the toys to behave themselves,' she answered primly.

I bet you are, thought Taryn. Poor kid.

She watched the little girl's serious profile. Serendipity had the kind of fine blond hair that was almost silver. Her pale eyebrows and eyelashes made her look permanently surprised.

Taryn decided to try again. 'Where do you go to nursery?'

'I don't. I go to work with my mother and help her.'

Taryn nodded, hiding a little smile – Mrs Garrance must have child-care facilities at her department.

'Would you like me to read you a story?'

Serendipity nodded.

'Then we'd better put the toys to bed – '

The little girl giggled. 'They're only toys, they

don't sleep!'

Taryn grinned. 'I forgot!'

They put the toys away and Serendipity selected a book. Taryn sat next to her on the bed and opened the first page, thinking it couldn't hurt to read to her – surely her mother wouldn't disapprove of that.

In her best story-telling voice, Taryn tried to make the educational book about shapes and colours sound interesting. There were no fairy tales in Serendipity's bedroom, Taryn noted. What a shame, no fun, no games, just sensible educational things.

Taryn closed the book. 'Bedtime.'

Serendipity's pale face grew worried and she glanced towards the window.

'What is it, Sweetheart?' Taryn asked, with ready sympathy.

'It comes to the window. It tries to get in.'

Taryn shivered – the child was so serious!

'Oh, Pet.' She gave Serendipity a quick hug. 'There's nothing out there.'

She went to the window and looked down into

the small back yard, then over to the park. 'See, the park is empty and it's a straight drop to the ground from your window. Not even a cat could climb it!'

Movement caught Taryn's eye. She could have sworn something was slinking from trunk to trunk in the park.

Now she's got me seeing things! Taryn thought.

'Just to make you feel better, I'll check that the window is shut and locked.' She made a production of pushing the sliding aluminium window closed until it clicked, then easing the little metal catch across so that it couldn't be opened. To cap it off she pulled the blind down, shutting out the cold, wet night.

'There,' Taryn turned and smiled at Serendipity. 'Nothing can get in now. Would you like me to leave a light on?'

Serendipity nodded.

When Taryn gave the little girl a kiss she was surprised by the way her small hands clung. She's really frightened, Taryn thought. How could that mean mother shut her in the dark!

She felt justified in leaving the hall light on and

the door ajar. That was when she noticed the bolt up high on the door of Serendipity's bedroom. Outrage flooded her. How awful! Did Serendipity's mother bolt her in?

She went downstairs to the blue and white kitchen and put the cordless kettle on, still feeling annoyed on the little girl's behalf. While she boiled the water to make a hot chocolate for herself, she wondered if a warm drink would help Serendipity sleep.

Taryn was about to suggest it when the back of her neck tingled. She grew still as she sensed a presence behind her. Someone or something was on the stairs!

'Please?' a little voice whispered.

'Oh, Pet!' Taryn muttered with relief. Now she was getting spooked! 'Look, you're supposed to be in bed – '

'I'm scared – '

Taryn put her hands on her hips and rolled her eyes.

Serendipity smiled, stepped off the bottom stair and ran across the tiles, slipping her cold hand into Taryn's. She turned her pale face, her large ice-blue eyes wide with fear, up to Taryn. 'Don't leave me.'

'Ah, Pet!' Taryn wasn't made of stone. Surely a little kid being left with a babysitter for the first time deserved some indulgence?

Taryn dropped to her knees, so that she could look Serendipity in the eye. 'I tell you what. How about I make you a nice warm milk? I'll bring my hot chocolate and I'll sit on your bed and read my book till you go to sleep, OK?'

The little girl's face glowed with relief.

Taryn hugged her. 'Now up to bed.'

The child shook her head solemnly.

In the end, Serendipity stayed with Taryn until the hot drinks were made, then they both went up the stairs. It wasn't as warm up in the bedroom. Taryn was glad of her hot chocolate.

After plumping up Serendipity's pillows so the child could sit and sip her warm milk, Taryn slipped off her winter boots, tucked her feet under her and curled up on the end of the bed. Hot chocolate in one hand, she opened her book with the other.

'Now I'm going to read. You're supposed to be asleep,' she informed Serendipity sternly.

The child nodded and smiled confidingly, a moustache of milk on her upper lip. Taryn could have hugged her. Instead she left her book face down on the bed and took the empty milk glass, placing it on the bedside table.

'Sleep now.'

Serendipity snuggled down under the covers. Taryn sipped her hot chocolate and picked up her book, resuming her place in the story. She was vaguely aware of Serendipity's serious little face watching her, but she wasn't going to encourage any more nonsense, as Mrs Garrance would have said.

A sharp hissing noise followed by a short howl startled them both. Serendipity's eyes flew to Taryn's.

'Only cats fighting,' Taryn said firmly, though her heart was thudding in her chest.

She looked down at her book, pretending to read. The words blurred in front of her eyes as she strained to hear any faint noise from the yard, but nothing came and soon she was involved in the story again.

In a few minutes Serendipity's breathing assumed the regular pattern of sleep. Taryn drained her hot chocolate and eased her feet off the bed. The little girl was fast asleep, one hand near her mouth as if the thumb might slip in. Smiling to herself, Taryn pulled the covers over her new friend and collected the empty milk glass.

Chapter **Three**

Because Serendipity had been so frightened, Taryn left the bedroom door ajar when she padded lightly downstairs. It always felt funny alone in someone else's house. She rinsed the mug and glass and put them in the dishwasher, then dried her hands and looked at the clock.

Another two hours until she could expect Mrs Garrance home. Should she curl up in the living room and read?

A dog howled, the mournful sound hanging on the cold night air. Taryn winced, hoping the sound wouldn't wake Serendipity.

When she leant across the kitchen sink to pull the blind down, she went cold. What was that darker shadow against the far wall? Why did it have a sense of stillness, of waiting?

Taryn gave herself a mental shake. Now she was making herself as spooked as Serendipity – it was probably the wheelie bin!

She tugged the blind down and picked up her book, intending to curl up in the living room.

An almighty clatter right outside the kitchen window made her leap sideways across the tiles, her heart in her mouth.

'Good Grief! What was that?'

It had sounded like wood and crockery breaking.

'Probably that silly cat, knocking over some pot plants,' Taryn told herself, but she didn't open the door to check. It was safely locked and it was going to stay that way!

A muffled cry came from upstairs.

'Blast!' Taryn muttered. Now she'd have to reassure Serendipity all over again.

She ran lightly up the carpeted steps and headed for the bedroom door. Suddenly the hairs on her skin lifted as an eerie, high-pitched whimper came from the bedroom.

Her feet turned to lead and she had to force herself to go on.

'Poor little soul,' she muttered, striving to control her instinctive reaction. If she was scared, no wonder Serendipity sounded terrified!

Taryn opened the bedroom door and went across to sit on the bed. Serendipity had pulled the covers right over her head.

Taryn had to smile. 'Don't cry – '

To her surprise Serendipity threw back the covers and sat up, hiding her face in Taryn's chest.

'There, there, Pet. Don't be afraid. I'm here – '

'It's there!' Serendipity moaned. 'It's at the window – '

'Nothing's there.' Taryn stroked the child's head, feeling the tension in her small, trembling frame. The poor little thing was totally spooked. Taryn could feel her own heart racing in sympathy. 'Your bedroom is on the second floor. Nothing could climb up.'

It was time to take control. Taryn prised Serendipity's arms loose and got to her feet. 'I'll show you there's nothing to be afraid of – '

'No!' The little girl clutched the covers and pulled them over her head.

Taryn almost laughed, but instead she used her best babysitter voice. 'Now, Pet, look up and see.'

She crossed to the window and waited until the fair head peeped over the covers, then she tugged on the blind, letting it spring up.

Serendipity's eyes widened and her mouth opened in a soundless scream.

Taryn sprang back in terror. Right in front of her loomed a massive head. Dark and bestial, it rested on huge shoulders. And, there on the sill, she saw the glint of long talons.

A feral gleam lit the creature's eyes. Taryn sensed malevolent intelligence as it looked up into her face.

She caught a ragged breath and staggered backwards until she felt the bed behind her knees. She sat abruptly.

Serendipity whimpered.

'It can't get in. The window's locked.' Taryn heard her own impossibly calm voice.

They winced as the metal window catch scraped on the aluminium frame.

If it's on the other side of the window, Taryn fought her disbelief, what's moving the catch?

Serendipity moaned when the window flexed in its frame and slowly eased up, as if opened by an unseen force.

The creature looked across at Taryn. She saw a flash of yellowing teeth, sensed the mockery of a smile.

Taryn reacted. Scooping Serendipity up in her arms, she ran out of the bedroom, slamming the door behind her.

Her heart thudding in her chest, she stopped across the hall from the door and tried to catch her breath.

The bolt!

Dumping Serendipity unceremoniously onto the floor, Taryn darted across and shot the bolt home. So that was why it was there – no, that would be ridiculous.

What *was* that thing?

At least they were safe now.

Taryn stood, panting, at the bolted door.

Serendipity clutched Taryn's left hand, trying to drag her away. Her breathless little pleas were hardly audible. Taryn became aware of an intense cold at her feet and looked down to see her sock-covered toes. A fierce chill was seeping under the door – she could feel it creeping up her legs. She looked down into Serendipity's white face.

The child's breath misted. 'Come away from here!' she moaned.

Taryn froze as the door handle turned, first one way then other.

If the creature could open closed windows, Taryn realised, it could slide back the bolt. She swallowed and tried to sound calm. 'I think we'll go now, Pet.'

It unnerved her to see how her breath misted

too. Even in winter in Cornwall, an open window didn't make a room *that* cold *that* quickly. And it certainly didn't make your breath turn into a heavy fog within a single heart beat.

With shaking hands she pulled a little side table across the top of the stairs. Serendipity watched her solemnly. She didn't ask what Taryn was doing or why.

The table wouldn't slow the creature for long. A spiralling surge of panic threatened to engulf Taryn. Her knees felt weak as she ran down the steps with the little girl at her side.

They came to a stop at the foot of the stairwell. Should they run left, through the living room into the street, or right, into the kitchen?

She didn't know what to do!

Taryn found Serendipity looking up at her, frightened but trusting. She took a firm hold on the little girl's hand – and on her self-control.

'We'll call your Mum first.'

In the kitchen, Taryn lifted Serendipity onto the servery bench and punched in the mobile phone number. She patted the little girl's thigh reassuringly.

'We'll be all right. You'll see.'

The child fixed ice-blue eyes on Taryn. Her baby teeth chattered with fear.

Taryn rubbed Serendipity's back, trying to stop that awful teeth-chattering. The phone rang and rang.

'Come on! Answer … Er, Hello, Mrs Garrance? It's Taryn here. I'm sorry to interrupt your meeting but …' Here Taryn paused. What should she say? No one would believe her story. She didn't believe it! 'Er, we've got trouble – '

'Did you leave the light on? Did you encourage her – '

'She was scared. I couldn't shut her in the dark–'

'I told you not to let her – '

Taryn rolled her eyes. 'Something is in the house with us – '

'Damn!' Mrs Garrance hissed, then a voice in the background at the other end said something Taryn didn't hear properly.

Serendipity's mother must have covered the phone because the voices became more muffled.

Taryn felt her cheeks flood with embarrassment.

Everyone at the meeting's probably laughing at me, she thought. She ground her teeth in frustration.

What was taking so long?

Taryn fought her panic. 'Mrs Garrance, what should I do?'

'Don't do anything,' the woman replied. 'There's nothing there – '

How can she say that? She isn't here! Taryn thought.

'But I saw the window open. I grabbed your daughter and ran out and bolted the door. I saw the handle turn – '

'Where are you now?'

'In the kitchen – '

Splintering wood shattered the quiet. Serendipity shrieked. Taryn gasped. 'It's smashed the table at the top of the stairs – '

'What?'

Taryn explained. 'I moved a table to slow it down – '

'You mean it smashed a table?' Mrs Garrance

repeated, astounded.

Someone at the meeting exclaimed. 'Class two manifestation, second-party witness – '

Taryn heard Serendipity's mother hiss. 'Quiet!' Then she addressed Taryn. 'Listen to me. There's nothing there. You are quite safe – '

'It's coming down the stairs!' Taryn gasped as Serendipity flung her surprisingly strong arms around her neck. Nearly strangled by the child's grip, Taryn gave up – the silly woman didn't believe her! 'I'm calling 999 – '

'Don't do that. You'll ruin everything. Hold on. I'm coming home.' Mrs Garrance cut the connection.

Chapter **Four**

Taryn gasped. She was alone with a frightened child whom she had to protect from something that didn't bear thinking about. She hung up the receiver and turned.

Her heart lurched.

She could tell by the shadow at the foot of the stairs that something huge was on the landing, halfway down the stairs.

Why was it waiting there?

Taryn lifted Serendipity off the bench. Where should they run? How on earth could she defend them?

She'd never out-run it, not with Serendipity in her arms, yet she refused to abandon her. She could feel the child's heart beating madly against her own.

It was up to her to save the little girl.

Then she noticed the kettle. The water in it would still be hot. Taryn grabbed it and took Serendipity's hand, pulling her silently across the kitchen to the laundry door.

Her mouth dry with fear, she opened the door as quietly as possible.

It was a dead end!

The laundry was no bigger than a large cupboard with a small, fixed window which neither of them could squeeze through.

Taryn tugged Serendipity in after her and pulled the door shut, praying the handle wouldn't click too loudly. Fighting her panic, she put the kettle on the washing machine and lifted Serendipity into her arms.

She tried to control her breathing, to hear above the pounding of blood in her ears.

It was out there, searching for them.

'We'll be safe in here, Pet. It doesn't know where we are,' she breathed in Serendipity's ear.

The little girl nodded, her body clinging to Taryn's.

Then they both heard it – a horrible snuffling grunt.

The creature was smelling the air, searching for their scent.

Taryn's skin went cold, then hot, with fear. This was too much. This was more than she could manage – but she had to cope, the little girl in her arms depended on her.

Something blocked the kitchen light which seeped under the laundry door. Taryn knew the creature was just outside, snuffling, sniffing, seeking their scent.

Serendipity's arms tightened impossibly around Taryn's neck until her head buzzed. She fought to ease the child's grip, to catch her breath. She needed to think!

The creature wasn't just a mindless animal. She'd seen that mocking expression as it looked through the window. Worse, it had the advantage of strength, of an animal's keen sense of smell – yet it had to have some weakness. But what?

Sickening fear churned in Taryn's belly as the door handle turned.

There was no lock on the laundry door, nothing to stop the creature entering. They were trapped!

With frantic, shaking hands she pulled the little girl's arms away from her neck. 'Get in the laundry tub, crouch down. Whatever happens, don't move.'

Taryn shoved Serendipity down, then covered her with a towel. She grabbed the kettle, squeezing the handle to hold the lid open.

The door clicked as the catch released. Serendipity moaned. Taryn lifted the kettle in an arc behind her to get a good swing.

Slowly, very slowly the door opened inwards. The creature stood silhouetted against the kitchen light. Grunting with the effort, Taryn flung the kettle's contents at the shape that loomed before her.

Behind her a child's scream tore the air. In front of her the creature dropped to the floor, writhing in pain. Taryn watched in sick fascination as it seemed to lose substance – to dissolve – like the wicked witch when Dorothy doused her with water.

Stunned, Taryn stared as the outline wavered. Beyond, no, through it, she could see the kitchen tiles.

What was happening?

This didn't make sense. Was the creature real or not?

Serendipity moaned.

No time to think!

Without turning her back on the thing, Taryn threw the towel off Serendipity and plucked her from her defensive crouch in the laundry tub. Heart hammering in her chest, she skirted the huddled, hazy outline that was the creature.

A strange keening groan came from it. No, wrong again. The groaning was coming from Serendipity.

Taryn hugged her closer and fled through the kitchen, past the stairwell and into the living room.

'We're going to be all right, Pet. We're going to get away,' Taryn told her, confident for the first time.

Serendipity arched her back, pushing away from Taryn. 'You hurt me!'

Taryn didn't know what she was talking about. 'I saved you. Saved us!'

She fought to hold onto the child, who suddenly writhed in her arms, struggling to get down.

'No!' Taryn cried, staggering. She didn't need this now. In desperation she slung the little girl over her shoulder in a fireman's hoist. Small feet kicked her viciously in the stomach, little fists thumped her lower back.

Taryn gritted her teeth. 'I'm trying to save you. You silly child!'

'Let me go!' Serendipity squealed. 'I'll get you! I'll let it get you!'

'Shush!' Taryn twisted the front-door handle, releasing the lock, and flung the door open as she glanced back over her shoulder. To her horror, the creature was lurching through the stairwell towards

them, staggering drunkenly from wall to wall.

'I hate you!' Serendipity yelled at Taryn. 'Let me go!'

Taryn charged out the door and down the front steps. It had been raining and the footpath was wet. Her socks were quickly soaked; her feet bruised by the rough surface.

For an instant she stood poised on the footpath with the reluctant child slung over her shoulder. Which way should she run? To her right was darkness and empty streets, to her left, lighted shop fronts and a car approaching.

'Thank God!' Taryn moaned. She ran, trying to wave one arm and hold onto Serendipity at the same time.

The car's headlights transfixed them then swept past as it continued on. Taryn could have wept with frustration. Her feet ached with cold, throbbed from running on the hard ground.

She darted around the high brick fence on the corner and swung Serendipity off her shoulder. Bent double, she tried to catch her breath.

'I hate you!' the child hissed.

Taryn blinked. Serendipity's face was twisted with malice, looking alien under the yellow glare of the street light.

'It's coming after you now,' the little girl smirked. 'It's angry with you now!'

Taryn sucked in her breath as the realisation hit her, and all this time she'd been trying to protect Serendipity! Mrs Garrance's words returned to her: no nonsense, don't indulge her.

Taryn refused to believe it. 'W...What do you mean?'

Her skin went cold with fear as Serendipity turned and beckoned to the creature, which was crouched at the corner, almost as if awaiting her orders.

Taryn gasped. It loped forward as if it had been waiting for the little girl's signal.

She straightened, stunned. Serendipity wasn't the victim!

'No,' Taryn croaked. 'I looked after you – '

'You hurt me – '

'I never meant to hurt you. I was only trying to protect you. It was after both of us.'

The creature hesitated, its massive head turning from the child to Taryn as if it was confused.

Serendipity's controlling it, Taryn thought, but she wasn't before. She was scared. What if she loses control again? It will turn on both of us.

Taryn knew she had to protect the little girl, even from herself.

She grabbed Serendipity, holding her small form against her chest. She backed slowly down the footpath. The creature shuffled after them, snuffling at their scent.

'We have to get away, Serendipity,' Taryn whispered in the child's ear. 'You must believe me. I wouldn't hurt you for the world, but this thing might – '

'It comes after me. Mummy says I must be stronger than it,' Serendipity's voice rose on a note of fear. 'But I'm scared!'

As if on cue, the creature charged forward. Taryn turned and ran, every muscle straining, her heart hammering with the effort. She could hear the creature's grunting breath, hear its taloned paws hitting the ground.

The lights of an approaching vehicle swung around the corner. Desperate, Taryn ran onto the road. As the car swerved to miss them the tyres screeched.

Panting with relief, Taryn staggered towards it.

The doors opened. 'Serendipity!' Mrs Garrance cried, pulling her from Taryn's trembling arms.

'It's after us!' Taryn gasped, each breath burning in her chest.

'Nonsense!' Ms Garrance snapped. 'Look!'

Taryn turned. The creature hesitated under the street light. Already it was losing substance.

'There's nothing there. Nothing, Serendipity!'

'Nothing,' the little girl repeated and as she spoke the creature winked out of existence.

Taryn gasped.

She had hardly caught her breath when a man's hand directed her insistently into the back seat of the car. The doors slammed shut.

Taryn sank back against the car seat and the man gave her a reassuring pat. As they drove around the corner she strained to peer over her shoulder – the street was empty. Mrs Garrance was right, there was nothing there.

The car stopped outside the Garrance's townhouse. Taryn watched as the mother climbed out and took Serendipity's hand. They walked up the short path to the door.

Two men hustled Taryn inside. Suddenly, she felt like a prisoner.

Chapter **Five**

By the time they had entered the living room Serendipity was seated on the deep couch like a little doll, her hands clasped in her lap, her small feet sticking straight out.

'Sit down, Taryn,' Mrs Garrance ordered.

Taryn sat. The two men glanced at Mrs Garrance and she nodded towards the security camera which was trained on the couch.

They were being filmed, Taryn realised. Maybe they'd filmed everything that had happened. Maybe they'd watched it, safe somewhere. Anger made her sit up. 'We were nearly killed – '

'Check the upstairs, Bob. Look for physical evidence.' Mrs Garrance placed a straight-backed chair in front of Taryn and sat opposite as if to study her reactions.

Taryn frowned. Physical evidence?

'You didn't follow my instructions, Taryn – '

'You were watching us!' Taryn accused. 'You set me up! Now I'm beginning to understand. Your daughter's gifted. I know Serendipity means Lucky Accident! I'm not stupid – '

The man who had patted her in the car gave a snort of amusement. Taryn looked at him, furious.

'Well, Bob?' Mrs Garrance asked as the other man returned from upstairs.

'The window is open, the door's open and there's a table ripped to splinters – '

The seated man gave a grunt of surprise. 'My God. It's never left physical evidence before -'

'Don't swear in front of my daughter,' Mrs

Garrance snapped. She turned back to Taryn, pinning a smile on her face that didn't fool the girl for a minute. 'It really is most unfortunate, Taryn. I didn't expect trouble. You're right, you were recorded. I film everything, for the record. The minute we knew you were in physical danger we came – '

Taryn didn't want to ask, but she had to know. 'What was after us?'

The adults exchanged looks.

'We're not sure,' one of the men answered.

Taryn liked his voice, he was friendlier than the others. He gave a quick grin of apology. 'We think it is the physical embodiment of Serendipity's fear . . . '

'I see . . . ' Taryn glanced at them and realised they were watching her closely. 'That's why she was able to banish it when you told her to?'

Mrs Garrance nodded and stiffened imperceptibly. 'It's a matter of self-discipline.'

She's afraid of Serendipity, Taryn realised. The mother was afraid of what would happen when her daughter no longer did what she was told. Would she turn on her mother one day? She had nearly done that with Taryn tonight.

'When I threw hot water on it, why did it fade away?'

'You hurt me!' Serendipity announced, remembering her resentment.

Ms Garrance flicked on the standard lamp and gasped as a series of red blisters were revealed on the child's shoulder, neck and cheek.

Taryn gave a moan of horror. Physical pain curled in her stomach. She lifted her hands to Serendipity's slender shoulders.

'Oh, Pet, I'm so sorry!' Hot tears rolled down Taryn's cheeks. 'I didn't realise. I wouldn't hurt you for the world.'

Taryn felt a hot flush run through her fingers, almost as if it was drawn out of her by the little girl. Suddenly, she heard the adults gasp.

Bob pulled Taryn to her feet and Mrs Garrance turned Serendipity to the light. The little girl's skin was now unmarked.

'Did you do this?' she asked the child.

Serendipity shook her head. 'Taryn let me do

it. She helped me.'

'What?' Bob released Taryn abruptly.

She felt the three adults turn and look at her. She swallowed and shook her head just as someone knocked at the front door.

Mrs Garrance glanced at her watch. 'It's Taryn's mother.'

She took Serendipity by the hand. 'Thank Taryn for looking after you and apologise for scaring her.'

Taryn accepted the child's apology in a daze. Mrs Garrance opened the front door and welcomed Taryn's mother as if nothing had happened.

'No problems?' Mrs Hewitt joked.

'Not a thing. Can I ask you something?' Mrs Garrance gave Taryn's mother that special look which said 'alone'.

'Wait in the car, Taryn.'

She walked down the path and climbed into the front seat, still too numb to feel anything.

After a moment her mother joined her. Mrs Hewitt started the engine then smiled at Taryn as Mrs Garrance waved and closed her front door.

'Well, aren't you lucky! And you thought you wouldn't be able to find a holiday job. Even better, Mrs Garrance has offered you a place in her department – '

'No, Mum!'

'I'm not having an argument, Taryn. You have to learn the value of money. You start at the P.R.D. first thing tomorrow morning.'

'P.R.D?' she echoed. 'That's where Mrs Garrance works. But what do the letters – '

'P.R.D? Why, the Paranormal Research Department, silly girl ...'

AFTER DARK

For details of other chilling
After Dark stories,
read on...

The Pipe
by James Moloney

"The taxi turned off the main road onto a bridge and I looked down, expecting to see a railway line, but instead I saw a stormdrain. It cried out for a skateboard. I sat up to get a better view. That was when I saw him, just that glimpse of legs and feet but enough to hint at a boy my own age, stooping, waiting inside the lip of a huge pipe that protruded from the wall of the drain. I was sure I saw a skateboard resting against his thigh ..."

There's something about the pipe that draws the skateboarder to it. 'Don't go in there,' the local kids warn, but those smooth concrete walls, curving away into the darkness, are the ultimate challenge to any skateboarder ...

The Lie
by Philip Neilsen

"Edward walked onto the bridge. He stopped in the middle, took a deep breath, climbed up on the rail and stood there, clutching the thick grey cable beside him. Lights were shimmering on the river's surface. It seemed more friendly at night, much more inviting. He looked at the part of the bank where the rocks were. There were only vague patches of darkness and he thought he could make out a shape on the rocks – a shape like a head and shoulders. He shuddered. He really should try to control his imagination …"

Edward tells a lie that even he begins to believe. After all, what matters is that all the kids at school – especially the beautiful Natasha – think he's a hero.
But only at the bridge will the truth come out, and making the wrong choice could be fatal …

The Snake Man
by James Moloney

"Terry would have turned to stare at the taxidermist's house again if a van had not pulled into the street, speeding towards them. It was slowing down by the time it passed Liam and it came to a halt only a few metres away from Terry. Two men spilled from the doors on either side.

'This the place, then?' asked the shorter of the two men. 'Don't like the look of those stairs. This box is pretty heavy.'

The second man was as slim as the other was fat. He stood by the back of the van, his hand on the large wooden crate inside, as his tiny eyes searched the street..."

Is it a crate or a coffin that Terry and Liam help to carry into the taxidermist's house? And is it merely coincidence that Terry disappears so soon afterwards? Or has he become a specimen himself ... ?

Other books in the *After Dark* series